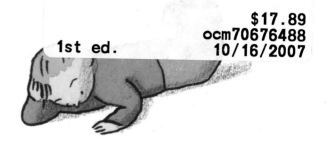

A big fat kiss to Joanna Cotler, and a thank you to
Jean de Brunhoff for my utopia: Celesteville.
—M.R.

Phooey!
Copyright © 2007 by Marc Rosenthal
Manufactured in China.   All rights reserved. No part of this book may be used or reproduced in any manner
whatsoever without written permission except in the case of brief quotations embodied in critical articles and
reviews. For information address HarperCollins Children's Books, a division of HarperCollins Publishers,
1350 Avenue of the Americas, New York, NY 10019.
www.harpercollinschildrens.com

Library of Congress Cataloging-in-Publication Data
Rosenthal, Marc.
    Phooey! / Marc Rosenthal.— 1st ed.
        p.   cm.
    Summary: A boy who claims there is nothing to do spends his day being anything but bored.
    ISBN-10: 0-06-075248-3 (trade bdg.) — ISBN-13: 978-0-06-075248-4 (trade bdg.)
    ISBN-10: 0-06-075249-1 (lib. bdg.) — ISBN-13: 978-0-06-075249-1 (lib. bdg.)
    [1. Boredom—Fiction. 2. Humorous stories.] I. Title.
PZ7.R719446Pho 2007   2006020218
[E]—dc22   CIP
                                                                                          AC

Typography by Neil Swaab   1 2 3 4 5 6 7 8 9 10   ❖   First Edition

PHOOEY!

by Marc Rosenthal

Joanna Cotler Books
An Imprint of HarperCollinsPublishers

EVER

HAPPENS

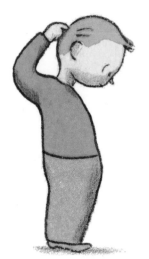